Al Katar

Other Books of Fiction

Pensacola Sharks
Captain Scratch Vol. 1-3
The Amazon Effect
The Last Warrior
Gator Restaurant
Country Line
G Corporation
Bus Ride
Meet Black People
Short Stories:
The Monkey
The Drop Off Zone
Third Strike
Stick Man
Education
Call of Duty, Two, Military Park
Call of Duty, G-Corporation
Call of Duty books are comprised of a
series of a lease three, but at this time at
least ten literary works in the making.

# CALL OF DUTY
## *PART TWO*
## *MILITARY PARK*

By

AL Katar

ISBN 978-1-957956-60-2 (Paperback)
ISBN 978-1-957956-61-9 (Ebook)

Inquiries and Book Orders
should be addressed to:

Leavitt Peak Press
17901 Pioneer Blvd Ste L #298,
Artesia, California 90701
Phone #: 2092191548

# CONTENTS

# INTRODUCTION

Call of Duty, part two, Military Park, hopefully illustrates computer generated humanity or human humanity when both clashes with modern day technology. What happens when we surrender our humanity to technology. About the consequences of this action? It is a modern-day gamble, that we play every day in this world. Do we roll a seven or do we crap out! Characters in this novel as, they confront all, surrendered their humanity to technology without a suitable off switch. Your guest as a reader of this novel is as good as mine. So, sit back in your gaming chairs and engage Call of Duty, Part Two, Military Park.

# DISCLAIMER

This is a work of fiction. **Names, characters, business, events and incidents are the products of the author's imagination.** Any resemblance to actual persons, living or dead, or actual events is purely coincidental.

# MR. WILDER
# FIRST WARRIOR

Let me introduce the five main characters of this storyline. First Mr. Wilder is a devoted video gamer; he knows all the tricks of the trade. He is a modern-day teenager with no full, or part time job. Mr. Wilder, he's a young 17-year-old kid; two months shy of his 18th birthday and soon to graduate high school. He has never taken on real life responsibilities; he has never had to pay a utility bill in his entire life or cut his own lawn.

His parents have given him in life everything that he has ever ask for most of the time. You can say Mr. Wilder is a spoiled brat. He has little regard for authority. He lives or resides in an upper class gated community.

Who has no real too little interaction with people of different nationality or people of lesser economic memes of support in their lives?

He's searching for the ultimate video game experience all of the time. Whatever new game comes to market that he can interact with in a metropolitan or urban environment; to where he is a suburban gangster with violent tendencies.

He loves are craves the power that comes with being an urban warlord in the 21$^{st}$ century. Without being responsible for the animated human characters within a video game. No video game is too violent within his humanity corridor. A sense of seeking, destroying or conquering the opponent within an urban environment is his ultimate search of conquest.

# MRS. JENNIFER SECOND WARRIOR

Mrs. Jennifer, the wife and mother of three kids, to which our next character works behind the counter of a fast-food restaurant; dealing with customers all day, but at night she escapes into the video gaming world seeking respect and confirmation of her worth as a human being by conquering Video game civilizations that she is the ultimate victor.

Also not be responsible for the cleanup of her actions. The ultimate high with out the ultimate responsibility of the human condition. This possibility has always existed within the virtual reality of a video gaming programs. She wants and seeks more out of this make-believe reality of video gaming.

# MR. MILLER
# THIRD WARRIOR

Mr. Miller, our third character is that executive in a successful Wall Street investment firm, that has done quite well for himself financially. He is on his second marriage with little time for romance. He's been a long-time video gamer, that engages with video gaming partners from around the world. He has the economic means of obtaining the best of gaming equipment as it is rolled out by the gaming industrial complex.

There is no link that he will not go to be satisfied within the gaming experience; without having to be responsible for his actions. Whatever he must do to be successful. Defending that gaming platform, no price is too high, even if it's humanity content maybe in question.

# MR. LEE
# 4ᵀᴴ WARRIOR

Mr. Lee, our 4th hero of Asian descent is a long-time video gamer, that celebrates the warrior class of his ancestral heritage. Any Asian conquest videos weather it's dealing with great battles of war between Asian countries from centuries pass. Such as the nations of China, Japan and Korean genre is his most favorite.

He even has a collection of samurai swords and costumes that he wears, to practices his warrior heritage most of the time, while playing his video games. He is seeking more and more conflict within the military combat video genre.

# MR. WILL
# 5TH WARRIOR

Our 5th member of this dramatic group of hero's is our combat veteran Mr. Will. He is single and is engaged to be married. His occupation is of a practicing attorney at a prestigious law firm. With many years of experience in the military. He has been deployed a number of times in the service of his country. He longs of being back on the front lines in real military engagements.

He long to be the warrior he used to be. Now as a civilian his military skills are not appreciated by some other people or corporations. He once served to protect people in faraway lands.

He's looking for more through video gaming, which allows him to rekindle past glories. It is an addiction at this time he cannot put past him. This addiction to military conquests has affected his relationships and interaction with other people. That others cannot gravitate too. He feels unappreciated and underserved in his society, where he's looking for the next video game high.

# BOOTS ON THE GROUND CORPORATION

Boots On the Ground Corporation, has been one of the leading video gaming manufacturers in the world. With offices and production facilities in several countries. They like any other corporation over time runs out of new gaming ideas. That reality does not increase their stock shares and shareholder value to their stockholders. They are looking for the ultimate game that will increase revenues.

Boots on the ground corporation, has come up to what they feel is the next great video gaming experience. They say let's give video gamers what they have been craving for the ultimate gaming experience. At the annual stockholders meeting they unveil this exciting and new concept called," Military Park". They have developed artificial intelligence and incorporated it into life size human looking robots of various nationalities. They have purchased several thousands of acres of land and will build a variety of different culturally diverse structural locations.

Boots On the Ground corporation, will outfit this new theme park for gamers. Video gamers will have a realistic experience with life size robots. These robots will be controlled through a system of routers station in secure locations. They will be programmed to interact with the human gamers and follow orders; to what the gamer wants them to do and achieve.

These robots will be program with a dos and don'ts programs. To whereby if they are told to do something outside of what is acceptable in humanities terms, toward another robot or person, they will disobey that order and ask for another order. That is in line with their artificial humanity program, to where they may do no harm to another robot or person participating in this gaming experience. Military Park is scheduled to open in one year.

This experience at military park is for those gamers that can afford the high cost of this experience. A bidding system must come into play to obtain a three-day experience in the military park community that they choose to visit and participate in, so let the games begin.

The Internet gaming world is advised of this new opportunity to experience the ultimate game to real life engagement with robot video characters. The Internet chat lines are ablaze and excited about this new opportunity. Millions of gamers are bidding to experience this new opportunity with all sorts of currencies including Bitcoin.

Months have passed while Military Park in being built. Within 30 days before the grand opening of military Park. Our five heroes receive an Internet email and cell phone message that they have been approved to experience the military park experience in person. The five are advised to participate in a one-day orientation of the facility before they participate in this new live experience.

They say goodbye to their loved ones, friends, and relatives with the hope of bringing back stories of a very good adventure.

The five heroes arrived at their local airport today, and de-part for Military Park in the middle of the country. Their airplanes land and they are greeted by a representative of Military Park. They all step onto a large tour bus, with the name "Military Park" on the side. After a short drive, they are escorted to their living quarters at the hotel on the same property of Military Park Control Center. Our five team members are excited to be part of the first group to experience this new gaming sensation. After a brief rest and lunching they are escorted to the orientation center. To where they see life size robots in military attire. Statues in authentic military attire for the era in which, they have each chosen to do battle in.

There are two spokespersons for the Military Park administration, one male one female, Miss Angela and Mr. Fremont are to explain what they hope to accomplish within this unique program why they are here.

They leave the briefing room and are escorted to a Control Center with large screens and computer desks that would rival NASA Control center. Miss Angela explains the environment of five different war periods. One being Asian conflicts, European conflicts, American Civil War conflicts, Urban and far Eastern conflicts.

The five group members are amazed at the quality of the life size acre ridge townships and battlefields. They asked the question; is this real or computer generated? Miss Angela the spokesman for the corporation says these are real; you can say movie sets. That we have develop over many acres of land that will give you the ultimate realistic combat experience; this is what you ordered and paid for.

Jennifer says to the spokeswoman Miss Angela what will keep us safe from the robots? What if something weird happens! Miss Angela says don't worry there are three low orbiting the earth satellites that monitor this facility and the robots.

You can say the humanity control function of the robots and the functions of this facility cannot be tampered with; because the control software program, it's not on earth, it's in outer space, in low earth orbit. Mr. Will says, can you explain what is defined, as low earth orbit?

Sure, Miss Angela says, low-earth orbit (often known as LEO) encompasses Earth-centered orbits with an altitude of 1,000 km to160 miles. For the purposes of the Commercial Use Policy, low-Earth orbit is considered the area in Earth orbit near enough to Earth for convenient transportation, communication satellites, observation and resupply, and no one can jump that high, our five heroes laugh!

You guys; we would like to call you five future warriors. Have until the morning to rest up and read up in your operational manuals at what you may expect, or the unexpected. Within each of your guest rooms you will be able to monitor the action as you see here in the control room until tomorrow morning.

After breakfast we will turn you guys over to wardrobe department and be fitted with that day appropriate military attire of that battle town or region you have already selected.

Once you are inserted within your battleground experience. You will have three days or 72 hours to experience and complete your mission that you guys already decided on. After this time, you will be recalled to an extraction area, and we will extract you by whatever means we feel is appropriate at that time. Whether you're on a mountain top or a pasture or any township square.

We will extract you and you will be placed back in the comfort of your hotel rooms. I encourage each and every one of you to get a good night's sleep of rest because your experience will be physically challenging. Each member of the group will return to their hotel room for a much-needed rest.

They each call home to family and loved ones to express their excitement to what they are facing for the next three days.

The next morning a 3:00 AM alarm sounds next to their beds. It's time to get up and prepare themselves for today's journey. The five-person group collect themselves and meet in the hotel lobby breakfast area. Along with other guests to fill their bodies with nourishment for the three days ahead.

At 5:00 AM a golf court cart arrives at the front of the hotel driven by spokesman Mr. Fremont, to transfer them to the wardrobe department for fitting. Each of our heroes are assigned two assistants to help them to be inserted into their war gear, as if they are preparing for a space launch.

There is a clock on a fitting room wall that is counting down the time left before they are inserted in their perspective combat zones or townships.

The clock says 90 minutes left to insertion, shows time 6:30 AM. They are each given a rifle or pistol that corresponds to their war Period that they have chosen in advance of them coming to Military Park; that fires an electronic blank bullet with extra ammo and various explosives. Such as hand grenades, a combat knife, compass, two-way radios and backpack of rations for three days.

Mr. Lee has been given a samurai sword for his time period. Being the 15th century in the far east. With 30 minutes remaining before insertion the five are escorted down five individual long and de-sending hallways as if they are going to be entering a large stadium.

Two words you think of in your mind! There is a "football crowd" on the other side of the large door in each one of our heroes' paths with one minute left before insertion. Their escorts wish them luck and hope to see them in three days, the countdown begins 10 9 8 7 6 5 4 3, the doors start to open to the sun rays are peeping through the doors, 2, 1 the doors are fully open. And our five heroes emerge into their individual combat zones that each one of them has chosen.

# MRS. JENNIFER INSERTION

Mrs. Jennifer enters her zone with noise deafening sounds of Gun fire and explosions. She immediately seeks cover behind a brick wall of a bomb out building. A Platoon of soldiers are already engaged in a firefight. To which, at this time; she does not know how to insert herself into the conflict; or what to do but, stay alive. Suddenly a female voice with a European accent signal to her to join her at a new position. Jennifer knows and realizes she is a robot that would be under her influence when told to do so.

Jennifer says to the robot what is your name? The robot says my name is Helen. Helen says what is your name? My name is Jennifer, what are we doing here? Helen says we are trying to prevent racial and ethnic cleansing by our neighbor country. They want to destroy our people; language and our way of life, we are battling them to the end.

Jennifer picks out a target and begins to fire her automatic machine gun at the enemy combatants that have a opposite color four-inch band on their arms. The enemy combatants that she engaged fall and reacts as if they're being hit by live ammo.

Jennifer is disabling a number of enemy combatants' and take chances of being hit herself, but she knows no harm will come to her because the returning fire is only computer generated with no effect on her body.

After 30 minutes of heavy fighting,there is a break in the fighting to where her unit is resting. Helen is assessing the wounded and casualties, so Jennifer and Helen, her computer robot comrade discuss more in depth about this conflict that she is embroider in.Helen introduces Jennifer to two other female freedom fighters, Dorothy and Ruth. Dorothy is a drone operator and Ruth is a sniper.

Jennifer says, I never heard of an women sniper. Helen says female snipers are the best because they don't kill for the sake of killing, they kill to protect the family unit.

# MR. MILLER INSERTION

Mr. Miller door is open, and he is embroiled in a World War Two battle for the Philippines islands. He is embedded with marines in a fierce gun battle and lands on a position that Mr. Miller is not really clear of the objective at this time. So, he just follows alone to what the other Marines are doing in assaulting the bunker embedded in the hillside.

Mr. Miller is ordered to move left to engage in crossfire at the bunker. Marines are being wounded all around him and enemy combatants are also taking heavy casualties. An energetics marine with a flame thrower takes on the bunker and destroys it. Other marines move up the hill as Mr. Miller platoon take a smoke break. Mr. Miller is introduced to Sergeant Wickham, to which he has a southern accent.

Sergeant Wickham says your part of that replacement crew buddy! The two men exchange small talk, as the sun goes down on the Pacific Island as the Marine unit dig foxholes and expecting a counter offensive that night.

# MR. LEE INSERTION

Mr. Lee on the other hand is introduced into a robust 15 century oriental village with people conducting business and a vegetable market place doing commerce with the local population. He is amazed by the calmness of the situation. He wanders around for a number of minutes and introduces himself to a young Asian woman by the name of Miss Dawn. They strike up a conversation over her township, but she informs him of impending danger of a warrior clan that wants to take over the village, enslave the peace-loving peoples and be under the thumb of the warlord name Woah.

All of a sudden, there is a commotion; Warriors with swords yelling wearing black as they are running toward the town square of commerce from behind Mr. Lee.

Another group of warriors emerge from passageways, and alleyways of the town square, wearing white with Samurai Swords out and ready for battle. Dawn says the black is the warlord Woah soldiers.

Mr. Lee pulls out his sword and prepares to do battle against the invaders and the two sides merge into battle. Mr. Lee is excited about fighting the enemy warriors. He knows nothing harmful will happen to him. He is fighting well, as the battle goes on for 20 minutes with casualties on both sides.

The enemy combatants retreat and leave the town as both sides are brewed and battered. Miss Dawn says they will be back, they always come back. They are regrouping; therefore, we must take this time to prepare for the next encounter. Mr. Lee is offered food and drink as he attempts to bond with his warrior fighting comrades.

# MR. WILL INSERTION

Mr. Will the fourth member of our dynamic group of eager fighters is inserted into a civil war battlefield engagement. He is wearing Yankee blue. As he assesses his position in a battlefield as the battle is raging. He is ordered to assist in the reloading of the cannon brigade. He follows the instructions of the Sergeant in charge. The Sergeant by the name of O'Reilly says to Mr. Will you're a new recruit; did they teach you anything before you got here?

Mr. will say no; I only joined up this morning, sorry! Sergeant O'Reilly says God forgive us! Do what I ask you to do and keep your head down, are you won't have it long.

After an hour of intense cannon fire by both sides the battlefield is still; with casualties all around as they are cared for.

The sun is going down over them their hills, as night is replacing day. A campfire is started to heat water for the doctors and cooking, as you can hear the wounded soldiers crying out for relief.

# MR. WILDER INSERTION

Mr. Wilder is inserted entering a downtown metropolitan area that is familiar with most people living life in a major metropolis city. There are many robot peoples of all ages and nationalities migrating in the downtown area. It is a very calm environment until a bank alarm sounds at the corner bank. Suddenly there is gunfire, and two bank robbers emerge from the bank, with bags of cash in hand. To which their getaway car pulls up and retrieves the robbers.

Mr. Wilder jumps into action, to participate in the chase; so, he jumps in an open top Jeep vehicle and pursues the bank robbers with his gun drawn.

Mr. Wilder starts firing his computer operated 44 caliber revolver pistol. The bank robbers return fire at Mr. Wilder. Mr. Wilder understands no harm will come to him from the robber's computer operated handguns. At high speed the chase is on in the city. There is no regard for traffic stops lights or people in crosswalks.

Even Mr. Wilder hits a pedestrian because, he understands the pedestrian is a robot.

Robbers' vehicle takes a fate far worse; as it goes airborne and lands upside down and the vehicle catches on fire and explodes; Mr. Wilder ends the chase, as he is amazed of the realism of the moment. There is another situation occurring on the sidewalk. A couple is being robbed at gunpoint and Mr. Wilder follows the robber or mugger down an alleyway.

Mr. Wilder points his gun and fire at the robber and the robber returns fire. Mr. Wilder shoots the alleged robber in the back, as he goes down and is dead. Mr. Wilder heartbeat is pounding his chest, as his adrenaline is very high.

Mr. Wilder wants more action as he takes an automobile at gunpoint from a citizen and begin to drive around town looking for more opportunities to involve himself in any violent occurrence.

Suddenly to Mr. Wilder delight there is a high-speed chase on the Interstate highway outside the city limits, with police cars already in pursuit. Mr. Wilder joins in the high-speed chase. He even bumps a few police cars, as he makes his way to the front of the chase. Two police cars have crashed and flipped on their side.

Mr. Wilder fires his weapon at the high-speed vehicle in front of him. The car he is chasing flies off the highway into a large body of water. The car immediately goes below the waves with no survivors. Mr. Wilder is excited and happy because of his heroic actions. A good day 1 of action. He returns to town to get a bite to eat. After dinner he checks into a Motel and rest for tonight; he is exhausted from the live action.

# BACK AT CONTROL CENTER

Back at Military Park Control Center, they have been monitoring the day's events of our five heroes. They are excited at the first day of Military Park activities. A very happy group of shareholders to the success of the new park.

They discuss having a bright future financially for their company on the first days; their stock price rose 22%. Military Park board of directors are celebrating in the boardroom with champagne for all, so tongues are loosened.

One board member says to the other, these five heroes just don't realize what they're doing for our company. They are more or less, Guinea pigs in our plans to become economically richer.

They don't realize that we have sold the screaming rights and that all gamers; millions of gamers are paying a subscription fee to watch them perform at this level of entertainment.

They've paid us to get richer through their efforts. We own the content of their work for future licensing. They will receive nothing, because we are an entertainment park.

Do you get paid after you leave an entertainment park? No, one board member replied, we have a great business model, drink up and be merry; the President CEO says, I will see you guys tomorrow.

All our heroes have bedded down for the night with two more days left in their paid experience. Mr. Will find a moment this evening to speak to Sergeant O'Reilly and say, how did we do this day.

Sergeant O'Reilly says both sides got a bloody nose, and I hope we can gather ourselves to be prepared for the next battle.

Mr. Will say to Sergeant O' Reilly, I know about the civil war; explain to me again, what are we fighting for. The Sergeant says, to keep the union together.

The other sides said, they want to fight for states' rights, whatever that is! Sergeant O'Reilly says to Mr. Will by the way, don't get captured because, they will return you to slavery or worse. Mr. Will without thinking says, I don't know about that. I'm a freeman, I've been free all my life! Sergeant O' Reilly says, I believe you but, you must be suffering from battle fatigue; get some rest it's affecting your memory.

# MISS JENNIFER
# SECOND DAY

The next day at 5:30 AM, the sun rises over Military Park. Our five heroes are finishing their breakfasts and preparing for that day's work of action adventure and life Learning. Jennifer's group is preparing to go on patrol to clear a nearby village or Township of enemy soldiers. Jennifer tells platoon leader Helen; she wants to be squad leader for today.

Helen says it's not as easy as it looks; you are responsible for the soldiers under your command and their wellbeing. I hope you can handle that. Jennifer says sure I can handle that.

As Jennifer squad or platoon makes their way through a forest and approaching the village they are ambushed. Jennifer men and women soldiers or falling like flies! Jennifer is shaken and frozen if you will.

Helen must interject herself back into the leadership position; remember Helen is controlled from the command center. Helen instructs the rest of her squad to keep firing back at the enemy combatants. Jennifer is ordered to move and assist the wounded.

Jennifer has no medical training, and she thinks to herself; I didn't have to worry about this in a video game. I just walked away and turned off the computer. I can't do that here now; my squad needs me to perform. After a short but bloody firefight.

The squad of robot soldiers gathers themselves and the robot soldiers are reactivated; remember these are robots not actual humans. Jennifer has gained a little live combat experience. Helen is not all that supportive of Jennifer, and she lets her know it, but they proceed on to the village.

Jennifer squad enters the village, so she gets a first-hand look of what war does to people. The village is bombed out with many homes destroyed.

Many people young and old scouting for food; graves are dug for those civilians who have been killed. The Look on people's faces, as they pray for the war to end, so they might have peace. Jennifer says to herself; I didn't have to deal with this with video games; I just press rewind, and everything is alright.

Helen tells the squad to set up a perimeter as they are sleeping in the village tonight. Jennifer says to herself only 24 hours left in my session; I'll be glad when it's over. I have gained a new perspective and responsibility to my humanity.

# MR. WILDER
# DAY TWO

Mr. Wilder, day two, after waking from a peaceful sleep he finds a diner and orders breakfast. After which he decides he wants a different and more violent situation on day two. He decides to travel outside of the inner city to the more impoverished and economic challenged parts of uptown. There he receives a first-hand look into lives of people on the other side of town, that most cities know, and have tucked away out of site. He sees people living in tent cities.

This environment is what he has seen on television, movies and or in video games. Mr. Wilder decides he will be the bad guy today. He will start the violence himself toward the people in the disadvantaged neighborhood side of Uptown. Because he understands that no harm will come to him.

Mr. Wilder goes into a bank and robs it. He pushes people down to the ground and tells them to get out of his way and dare someone to stop him. He fires a few shots into the ceiling of the bank. A bank guard returns fire and Mr. Wilder fires back at the guard and kills him. Remembering the bank guard is only a robot, that will be revived or re-booted later that day.

Mr. Wilder goes on a violent rampage of his own. Robbing stores, pawn shops and all types of businesses. He even comments a number of automobile car jackings. His heart rate is pumping very fast.

He even involves himself in a shootout with local gang members. Killing a number of them.

Mr. Wilder is bored from all the killing he has done. He goes for a bite to eat at the diner. There he meets a woman name Alice and her daughter Sally, as they develop small talk. Mr. Wilder ask Alice where she is living? Alice says for right now, we are living on the street.

She explains her eviction from her apartment after she lost her job. She is looking for another job, with health care and benefits, but has no childcare for her daughter at the moment.

Mr. Wilder invites the two of them to his motel room for the night. The family can have the bedroom, as he will sleep on the couch for tomorrow here, is his last day in town. She accepts.

Once at the motel Alice daughter is watching cartoons on television. Mr. Wilder and Alice discuss more in detail about his and hers life situations. Mr. Wilder gains more insight and respect for people that are economically challenged; compared to his life of privilege. They all three beds down for the night.

# MR. MILLER SECOND DAY

On the second day of Mr. Miller Pacific war enactment. The sun rises out of the Pacific Ocean, displaying a beautiful view but, the reality is much different. His squad is ordered to clear out any enemy positions on the mountain top. The enemy has a great view of anything moving below them and can direct their artillery fire with more accuracy down on the marines; too clear them out won't be easy but, it will be costly.

The firefight begins, men dying on both sides. Mr. Miller involved themselves in the fighting; he knows he cannot be injured, so he is putting on a great fighting performance worthy of a medal.

After the marines clear the mountain top, Mr. Miller is ordered to participate in a medical evacuation of a number of the marines. He helped carry more stretchers down to the medical tents. Men are moaning in pain; some have lost limbs, some have lost their minds, some are given last rites! Mr. Miller realizes there is no off switch here; there's no rewind button.

The consequence of war is everlasting to damage men and women and their family back home. He gains a new perspective and respect for what gaming is and what it is not! Mr. Miller is placed on guard duty that night expecting an enemy counterattack.

Later that night someone says the enemy is in the wire! They're breaking through the wire, gunfire erupts! Many tracer bullets are flying everywhere; the enemy is on the wrong side of the wire now. Mr. Miller is instructed to install his bayonet on his rifle. Mr. Miller says why me? I have only 24 hours left in this game. Sergeant says, I got you for 24 more hours so, I'm going to use you.

Mr. Miller finds himself in hand-to-hand combat. He's putting on a good show. He encounters and kill a number of the enemy soldiers keeping in mind but, they're only robots and can be reactivated anytime.

This fact keeps him from losing his mind over the waste of humanity. The hand-to-hand combat battle ends but, many soldiers are wounded and killed on both sides.

Mr. Miller just stares at a dead platoon leader corpse! Then another soldier says to Mr. Miller; you're in charge now! We have got a big day tomorrow you are our leader. Mr. Miller cannot sleep the rest of the night but, tomorrow will become his last day he says to himself, what's next!

# MR. LEE
# SECOND DAY

Mr. Lee, on his second day of combat is waken by Miss Dawn and given a bowl of rice for breakfast. They don't have much food in the village, but they are willing to share. Dawn invites Mr. Lee to her home where her mother and father still reside. Her father is missing one arm due to fighting warlords over many years. She has a younger brother that wants, one day to be a warrior like his father.

Mr. Lee observed many older men in the village missing lambs or body parts. The cost of war has no value button because the cost is too high to compute. Mr. Lee understands that these people are robots but, has a greater understanding of what war is and what it is not.

Gaming has two sides in the video gamer's mind. For all the losers and the winners, what have you lost and what have you won, that is the question? There is a knock on the door; an old woman says they're coming again, we must fight! Prepare yourself.

Mr. Lee and Dawn rush out to evaluate the situation. The wounded robots have been reactivated for more fighting.

This time the enemy is bringing more equipment to the fight. Ladders to scale the walls and battering Rams for the gates. The enemy is gathering itself about two miles from the village. They will not attack today, but by tomorrow is Mr. Lee last 24 hours in the war games, but there will be no good sleeping tonight for tomorrow the battle is on!

# MR. WILL
# SECOND DAY

Mr. Will second day, he is awakened by a young black American servant girl named, Miss Mary working for the blue bellies, as she was liberated some weeks ago as the northern troops captured southern territories. She is working in all manner of positions supporting northern Army units, such as cook, nurse and maid to the northern army staff.

Miss Mary tell Mr. Will, you wake up now and go to work or the boss man will be mad at you for being late. Sergeant O'Reilly instructs Mr. Will to join the artillery squad, as to they are moving the entire army unit further South.

Mr. Will joins the squad as they March with cannons to the next location. Mr. Will feet is starting to hurt in a big way; he falls behind the squad and says to himself, I didn't sign up for this. I'm going to outsmart them, go into the woods and rest my feet.

Mr. Will does just that; he takes off his shoes and cools his feet in a nearby lake of water. Then he takes a lay down position in the woods and falls asleep as time passes.

He is awakened by the rifle butt of a confederate soldier, saying you're my prisoner boy!

Mr. Will is ordered to put on his shoes and follow the soldier at gunpoint. Mr. Will arrives at the confederate camp where he is put to work supporting the southern Army. He meets other black Americans there supporting that confederate army unit. Confronts a black male slave named Mr. Fred and a black female by the name of Marilyn. Fred tells Mr. Will he's not working hard or fast enough; you're going to get all of us slaves in trouble.

Mr. Will regrets his mistake of not following his sergeant's orders, but understands as night falls, he only has 24 hours left in the gaming scenario. Mr. Will bed down for the night on the ground.

Mr. Will says to Fred, where is our tents? I had a tent last night, Fred says boy the tents are for the confederate soldiers, a slave sleeps on the ground on the battle grounds. Mr. Wills says, I'm not a slave; I'm a free man. Fred says you're dreaming, go to sleep or we'll all be in trouble.

# MR. WILDER
# DAY TWO

Mr. Wilder day two, after waking from a peaceful sleep he finds a diner and orders breakfast. After which he decides he wants a different and more violent situation on day two. He decides to travel outside of the inner city to the more impoverished and economic challenged parts of uptown.

There he receives a first-hand look into lives of people on the other side of town, that most cities how, have tucked away out of site. He sees people living in tent cities.

This environment is what he has seen on television, movies and or in video games. Mr. Wilder decides he will be the bad guy today. He will start the violence himself toward the people in the disadvantage neighborhood side Uptown. Because he understands that no harm will come to him.

Mr. Wilder goals into a bank and robs it. He pushes people down to the ground and tells them to get out of his way and dare someone to stop him. He fires a few shots in the ceiling of the bank. A bank guard returns fire and Mr. Wilder fires back at the guard and kills him. Remembering the bank guard is only a robot, that will be revived or re-booted later that day.

Mr. Wilder goals on a Violet rampage of his own. Robbing stores, pawn shops and all types of businesses. He even comments a number of automobile car jackings. His heart rate is pumping very fast. He even involves himself in a shootout with local gang members. Killing a number of them.

Mr. Wilder is bored from all the killing he has done. He goes for a bite to eat at the diner. There he meets a woman name Alice and her daughter Sally. ask day to develop small talk. Mr. Wilder ask Alice where she is living? Alice says for right now, we are living on the street. She explains her evicted from her apartment after she lost her job.

She is looking for another job, with health care and benefits, but has no childcare for her daughter at the moment.

Mr. Wilder invites the two of them to his motel room for the night. The family can have the bedroom he will sleep on the couch for tomorrow here, is his last day in town. she accepts. Once at the motel Alice daughter is watching cartoons on television.

Mr. Wilder and Alice discuss more in detail about his and hers life situations. Mr. Wilder gain more insight and respect for people that are economically challenged; compared to his life of privilege. They all three beds down for the night.

# BOARD MEETING SECOND DAY

The board members at Military Park meet again in the boardroom that next morning where they are still basking in the glow of their financial gain with confidence. The President of the board makes an announcement, ladies, and gentlemen he says; it is with great pleasure that I say these facts to you.

Unbeknown to our five heroes that they are making us richer by the moment. In addition, board members; we have sold for a large fee, the live gaming experience already to other peoples or gamers before our five heroes even arrived at our park.

Last, but not least, we are in the process of developing a video game titled "Call of Duty Two, Military Park". It should be a hit, with the millions of video gamers worldwide.

Other human gamers have been inserted over the last two days: without our five heroes' knowledge. They are thinking all of the characters besides themselves are robots, but there are many live humans playing parts.

No two humans know who's a robot and who's a human; that makes it more interesting.

This gives us a chance like no other to study their humanity to the situations they are involved in. That they are inserted into this study has increased our revenue stock price that has opened up another 25% at the opening of the New York Stock exchange. What a great day; what a great business model.

# THE LAST DAY

As night falls on our five heroes on the second day, they realize they only have 24 hours left before extraction. They have learned a lot about their obligation to humanity within themselves. They play it cool not to ruffle feathers of their host robots. Looking forward to going home and to be reunited with loved ones. They say the best laid plans of mice and men have known to go astray. Little did anyone know in the Western Hemisphere what was to take place to interrupt our five heroes' plans of being taken away from Military Park encampment.

A run away and lawless Republic In the eastern territories or hemisphere, has different plans for our heroes. They have developed a rocket that can't destroy satellites in low earth orbit. This fact is not well known in other parts of the world within other governments. The Republic that is firing the rocket wants to prove a point. They inform the rest of the world governments at 3:00 AM eastern standard time this day.

They will launch a new supersonic rocket to intercept a dead satellite in low earth orbit. So, the rest of the world will take notice and respect their Republic in their mind.

The rest of the world is alarmed by this test, especially other space agencies. NASA being one of them want this test not to go through they say. Don't these people understand that to destroy a satellite in low orbit will produce millions of pieces of debris; traveling at thousands of miles an hour and they may strike other satellites, and the low orbiting international space station (ISS), with astronauts aboard.

The Republic government has a 4:00 AM eastern launch time. That's when the dead satellite is in the best position over the earth to be destroyed. By the time other world powers are properly notified, it is too late to stop it.

The 4:00 AM countdown begins 10 9 8 7 6 5 4 3 2, the supersonic rocket engines ignite,1 the rocket lifts off from its launchpad.

NASA is tracking the rocket. It is on a collision course with the dead satellite. It will reach low earth orbit in 10 minutes. Then it will strike the dead satellite.

With a firetail existing the rocket with precision it strikes the dead satellite. A large explosion occurs; the dead satellite is now in a million pieces moving at thousands of miles an hour in lower earth orbit.

NASA has alerted the astronauts aboard the international space station to prepare for impact from some of the pieces of the destroyed satellite. The astronauts may have to abandon ship if there is significant damage to life support systems on the space station, they brace for impact!

A cloud of debris approaches the space station on bated breath. The astronauts are fearful to what may or may not happen. As satellite debris passes nearby the space station and moves away from the space station, luckily the space station was not hit by any of the debris.

But no such luck for Military Park satellites. Two of the three satellites controlled by them were struck with debris, disabling all command functions of Military Park automated systems. Even the elevators at the hotel are malfunctioning. The doors of Military Park control building are malfunctioning also, what's next!

The Military Park control room tries desperately to reinstate control over its systems at this point to no avail. Miss Angela is sleeping and in a good state of mind. Her cell phone rings by the President, CEO of Military Park and informs her of the mishap. Explains to her as long as the system is not under their control, no extractions will take place until then.

Our five heroes will just have to wait, Miss Angela says, how long? The President says, your guess is as good as mind, hours maybe, one day maybe, two days; they will have to endure.

All communications to their two-way radios for extraction are down for the moment. And will not work in the park. We are working on switching to another satellite but that takes time.

# MISS JENNIFER
# LAST DAY

Miss Jennifer awakens on her last day at military park. Helen has made Jennifer squad leader again. This time Jennifer is more focused on the wellbeing of the soldiers in her command. Today's assignment is to clear a village of enemy combatants. Jennifer and her squad arrive at the village two hours later.

They immediately engage in combat but, she noticed a difference in the enemy robots. Laying down, falling, they don't play dead.

They are standing and becoming aggressive toward her squad members; something is wrong, she says to herself. Helen realizes the same thing, our weapons are not working, but the enemy weapons are, something has gone wrong!

The robots from both sides or in hand-to-hand combat. They're tearing each other apart. Arms are coming off; legs are coming off; wires are everywhere; this was not part of the safety protocol.

Jennifer and Helen with the few robots they have left, decides to disengage from the battle and seek hard cover from the enemy robots. Unfortunately, on the way out of town.

Helen is struck in the head by a large rock. Helen goes down, Jennifer and other robots assist in her recovery from the battlefield to a safe position. Miss Jennifer realize Helen is bleeding from the head; she thinks to herself robots don't bleed.

Helen wakes up weak in the head and slow to speak. Helen says I'm not a robot; I paid good money to experience this video program. Mrs. Jennifer realize she must get help to Helen. She takes out her two-way radio and calls for help!

The radio is not working; no one is answering on the other end. Jennifer has had enough of this experience. She wants out of Military Park but, has to hold her position and care for Helen until help arrives.

# MR. MILLER'S LAST DAY

Mr. Miller, to his knowledge has 24 hours left in Military Park. He is asked to take a squad of men to clear a village of enemy combatants. As they enter the village, they are ambushed; a firefight occurs. Mr. Miller realize the shots from his gun is not working. The enemy combatant's robots are not falling are playing dead.

All the robot's soldiers on both sides are in hand-to-hand combat, tearing each other apart. Sergeant Wickham is stabbed with a knife or bayonet. Blood is coming from his wound. Mr. Miller pulls the Sergeant to a safe position with robots all around.

Mr. Miller says robots don't bleed! The sergeant says, I'm not a robot! I paid good money for this experience. Mr. Miller has had enough; he takes out his two-way radio and call for help but, there is no answer on the other side. He applies bandages to the Sergeant wounds. He cannot leave the Sergeant so, he carries him on his back to a safer location, hoping help is on the way.

# MR. LEE'S LAST DAY

Mr. Lee's last day as the sun rises over the village that he is preparing to protect from the hostile warlord Mr. Woah army. A trumpet sounds, another battle is about to begin, as the enemy army is at that the base of the wall of the village.

Mr. Lee and village town people drop heavy rocks on their heads. Yet the robots do not go down, they become more aggressive. Mr. Lee is perplexed and feel something is wrong.

He takes out his sword and uses it on one of the enemy soldiers climbing over the wall; it has no effect on him.

Miss Dawn is putting up a good fight also, but soon she is wounded in the shoulder and it's bleeding.

Mr. Lee takes her off to a safe location for the moment. Mr. Lee says robots don't bleed; Miss Dawn says, I'm not a robot! I paid good money for this video game experience.

Mr. Lee thinks about how many more of the park robots are actually human. Our team was not told that other humans were also in this video exercise.

Mr. Lee takes out his two-way radio because he has had enough, but there is no answer on the other end of the radio. Robots are taking other robots apart as he carries Miss Dawn back to her parents' home and puts a bandage on her womb. He has to wait for help to arrive whenever that is.

# MR. WILL
# LAST DAY

Mr. Will rises early on the last day of his gaming experience, and he is stiff in his neck. He complains, I'm have been sleeping on the ground, with only an ear of corn for breakfast. Mr. Will, Mr. Fred and Miss. Marilyn are put to work immediately doing hard work to assist the confederate army. The confederate army will be moving South; that means back to the plantation for these three black Americans; to which they are not looking forward to that, especially Mr. Will.

You can say Mr. Fred and Miss Marilyn are use to the hard work on the plantation. Mr. will convince his two workmates to attempt an escape. They decide to make a plan, as they are moving South and waiting for the right moment.

The moment has arrived as all three run into the woods. The confederate soldiers are very sore about their action as they pursued him.

They are fired upon as bullets pass by their heads. Mr. Fred yells out am hit! They see he is shot in his lower back as; they help him to a safe location.

He cannot move; he is bleeding and in great pain! Mr. Will say to himself, what robot bleed. Mr. Fred says I'm not a robot! I'm human and paid good money for this video experience.

Miss Marilyn says also; I'm not a robot slave, I'm human also, I also paid good money, I'm a video gamer.

Miss. Marilyn tears off a piece of her dress and makes a bandage for Mr. Fred to stop the bleeding. Miss. Marilyn says it's a good thing my job is a nurse, this is not what I planned for or imagine.

Miss. Marilyn has a two-way radio hidden under her dress; she's had enough and calls for the extraction team, but there is no one on the other end of the radio. They must survive till help arrives.

Now all of our five heroes understand that they're in a bad situation. They weren't told everything about their pending adventure at Military Park.

They feel as they have been used by Military Park corporation and for right now; there are hoping and praying that the radios will soon be working and the GPS inside the radios will give the extraction teams their locations when working. In the meantime, they have to hold on and survive.

# MR. WILDER
# LAST DAY

Mr. Wilder last day as the sun rises over the city. The hustle and bustle of the city and people along with the struggle of economically challenge people has had a humbling effect on Mr. Wilder.

He understands that life is not a video game, that you can pause or hit the rewind button. The three of them are having breakfast; afterwards they take a walk in the park. They take the time to feed the birds, as their having a joyful time together.

Suddenly from nowhere a man and woman team wants to rob them. Alice says she has no money to give them. Mr. Wilder and the man robber starts fighting. The woman robber pushes Alice to the ground, hitting her head on the sidewalk and cutting her forehead.

Mr. Wilder gets the better of the fight and the two robbers run away, but Alice is bleeding!

Mr. Wilder says, I did not know robot's bleed. Alice says, I'm not a robot neither is my daughter, we are both humans. Alice says, she won a contest, and the prize was three days at Military Park, all experiences pay at this time; I've had enough and want to go home.

They both call for evacuation from the town, but neither of their radio phones are working.

They find bandages for Alice headwound, but in the meantime they notice something is wrong with the robot towns people.

They are fighting amongst themselves and tearing each other apart. A robot approaches them, and Mr. Wilder fires his weapon, and the robot does not play dead.

They all three run and hide from the malfunctioning robots. Waiting for the radios to work and for help to arrive.

# BACK AT MILITARY PARK HEADQUARTERS

After the initial dust has settled at Military Park headquarters. Military Park President says all options are on the table. I'm getting control restored in some way to the military park robots. The spokesperson Mr. Fremont comes up with an idea.

Have us contact the Air Force; they have a rocket that can be fired from the belly of a jet aircraft; that can make itself into lower earth orbit.

We just have to program the software in the nose of the rocket. We can do this at the Air Force Base just outside of town. The quicker the Air Force plane arrives, the quicker our problem will be over.

The corporate board agrees to the plan. The world is waking up to what has happened to military park satellites. The park stock price is falling like a rock. The Air Force has agreed to take on the mission in restoring communications to Military Park.

Within two hours a special jet plane arrives at the Air Force Base and Military Park technicians go right to work installing the computer program in the nose of the rocket.

The world is waiting and praying that the rocket be fired from the belly of the jet plane.

The Air Force plane is ready for takeoff in record time. The plane has to reach an altitude of 40,000 feet before firing the rocket satellite. It will take another 45 minutes for this to happen. Back at the control room and in the boardroom, they can see on their televisions the chaos and confusion within Military Park.

The terrible things the robots are doing to other robots and chasing human beings that were embedded in the park.

The human gamers in the park are seeking safe shelter anywhere they can find a place, as the robots are searching for them.

The artificial intelligence chip in the two-way radios is giving away their positions unknowing to them. It's only a matter of time before they are located and found out to where their locations are.

The special Air Force jet plane is ready to take off from the runway, but the flight is placed on hold. NASA has called the Air Force and said you must wait; that debris cloud of metal is circling the earth right now.

It has to pass your launch location, or it may destroy the satellite as when it enters low earth orbit. The military park control room is besides itself, but they can only wait till the metal debris cloud passes by.

One-hour passes, the metal debris field has passed by, and NASA has given the ok for takeoff. The Air Force plane roars down the runway and liftoff with the fate of men and women, belief in humanity depending on a successful launch.

The plane reaches an altitude of 40,000 feet. The countdown begins to the launch 10 9 8 7 6 5 4 3 2 1 ignition launch. Fire erupts out of the back of the satellite rocket engine. It climbs straight up into the heavens. 45,000 feet 50,000 feet 60,000 feet. At 160 miles altitude, it arrives in low earth orbit.

The head of a rocket is separated from the motor or booster. The satellite emerges from the rocket and deploys itself, but the satellite must signal back to ground control that it is ready to receive instructions.

This will take an additional 10 minutes. People in the control room and company executives await in silence.

As the clock on the wall passes the 10-minute mark, no signal is received from the satellite 11 minutes pass, 12 minutes pass, just when they thought all was lost; a signal comes into the control room.

The satellite is ready to receive information. there is a roar from the control room and the boardroom! Information is sent up to the satellite and the satellite responses, it has received information.

At this point the two-way radios that human people were given will work; for how long we don't know. The control room starts calling all phones; the radio phones are ringing. All our five heroes answer their phones. Mr. Will explains they're dire circumstances and GPS information within the phones are also working.

A team of helicopters have been standing by for extraction.

Each of the many human gamers are instructed to move to a pickup location as they struggle with the wounded to get to the extraction points, but they do. Ask the helicopters approach the landing zones all is not well.

The robots are still walking or marching toward the GPS locator in all phones; as the five team members and their wounded are aboard the helicopters, they are instructed to throw away their two-way radios out of the helicopters.

With the look of joy and relief on the team members faces.

They are grateful to be airlifted to safety not knowing that there is a bigger problem ahead at military park Control Center. Doing the helicopter ride, Mr. Will notice that Mr. Wilder still has in his possession, his 44-caliber pistol.

Both men look at the weapon with sorry eyes!

Mr. Wilder gingerly throws the weapon out of the helicopter and say, it's not for me, at this time! They arrived back at military park and all five of our heroes are escorted the control room.

They learn that the satellite has not fixed all the problems associated with Military Park. Especially the robots; you have to understand the robots are still violent toward themselves and any living person. That problem has not been brought under control.

The robots are threatening to break containment and adventure outside of the park. This is a major danger to the major city Just miles from the park.

We have no other alternative, but to destroy the park in other words, "Nuke It" with a small non-nuclear wave bomb, that destroys only electronic components within a five-mile radius of the blast.

This action is already under way as we speak; all humans have been extracted from the park.

Someone in the control room said one minute to bomb drop. All five heroes, as all others are fixed to the closed-circuit TV screens. They see the plane approaching the middle of Military Park and drops its payload.

It hits in the middle of the park as a flash of light occurs as the non-nuclear bomb burns out all of the robots electronic components.

Less than a minutes after the impact, all robots fall to the ground, hopefully the nightmare of man's experiment of humanity has ended at military park.

You the reader of this novel must draw your own conclusion; to what has happened. Whether this be fact or fiction; man, and artificial intelligence can sometimes combine into a good thing or a lethal weapon, you the reader have to decide for yourselves!

# The End

Al Katar

Other Books of Fiction

Pensacola Sharks

Captain Scratch Vol. 1-3

The Amazon Effect

The Last Warrior

Gator Restaurant

Country Line

G Corporation

Bus Ride

Meet Black People

Short Stories:

The Monkey

The Drop Off Zone

Third Strike
Stick Man
Education
Call of Duty, Two, Military Park
Call of Duty, G-Corporation

Call of Duty books are comprised of a series of a lease three, but at this time, at least ten literary works are in the making.

# ABOUT THE AUTHOR

AL Katar was born a baby of the Civil Rights Movement in the mid 1950's. A child of the 60's. A man of the 70's and a storyteller of the 21st t century, who hasn't forgotten the great writers of the past. He writes in the action, suspense, drama, comedy and the everyday "just be real with me story" genre. From stories titled "The Last Warrior", "Gator Restaurant", "Third Strike", "Drop Off Zone", "The Monkey", "Pensacola Sharks", "Meet Black People" just to name a few and also a bonus feature "Education,

The Sitcom", Katar consider himself to be a transfer writer. Katar to his knowledge is the only writer to publish a three book trilogy on the black pirate "Captain Scratch". He is looking for representation in the film, book and entertainment industry. Katar hopes to build a meaningful relationship and partner with progressive Hollywood studios to maximize sales of a number of his books to be made into movies. He believes with the right management team and investment network the sky is the limit. Some wise person once said only when a writer is stretched and has suffered, that writer will become better. Katar is ready and willing to suffer and to be stretched all the more. See Amazon/AL katar/ Books.

AL Katar at Work

# Credits/Contributors

Education News Network (ENN)

Of Pensacola, Florida

Mr. Cedric (Cid) Langham

ENN Vice President Chicago, Illinois

Publicist

Patricia Ann Pryor

Country Line Music.Com

Song "My Heart" written by AL Pryor

Three Broke Comics.Com

Writing Staff

Scratch Kids Products

Bug Tubes

Spencer For Hire Graphics of Pensacola,

Florida, for front and back cover.

Avonbuynow.com